A GOLDEN BOOK • NEW YORK

Copyright © 1994 by the Estate of Richard Scarry
All rights reserved. Published in the United States by Golden Books, an imprint of Random House
Children's Books, a division of Random House, Inc., 1745 Broadway, New York, NY 10019, and in
Canada by Random House of Canada Limited, Toronto. Originally published in slightly different form
by Random House Children's Books in 2004. Golden Books, A Golden Book, and the G colophon are
registered trademarks of Random House, Inc.
randomhouse.com/kids
Educators and librarians, for a variety of teaching tools, visit us at RHTeachersLibrarians.com
Library of Congress Control Number: 93073767
ISBN 978-0-307-16803-0
MANUFACTURED IN CHINA
32 31 30 29 28 27

It's a fine morning in Busytown.
Everyone is rushing to work.
Let's see where they're going.

Richard Scarry's
BUSY, BUSY TOWN

Office Workers

Many people work in offices, like this lawyer. If two people have an argument, lawyers try to settle it.

There are all kinds of writers. The best writers write children's books.

PUBLIC LIBRARY

Librarians lend people books from the library. The best librarians are children's book librarians.

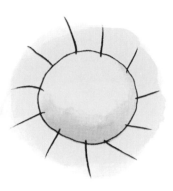

Artists paint pictures. The best artists paint pictures for children's books.

The best window washers do not drop their pails of water!

This is a bank. We keep our money here, where it will be safe.

A guard stands by the door of the bank.

Messengers quickly deliver packages to offices all over town.

On Main Street

There are all kinds of shops and stores on Busytown's Main Street.

You can wash your clothes. Oh, dear! The washing machine is leaking.

Water is coming out of the laundromat.

You can get your shoes fixed.

You can buy candy and books.

On Main Street you can buy medicine, tools, apples, and oranges. You can even get a haircut.

At the Post Office

Huckle writes a
letter to Grandma.

He takes it to the post office, where a postal
worker weighs the letter. Then the postal worker
puts a stamp on the letter. Another postal worker
uses a rubber stamp to cancel the letter. Now the
letter shows the date it was mailed.

A sorter puts all the letters going
to Grandma's town in one bag. All
the other letters go in other bags.

The mail truck driver takes
the mailbags to the airport.

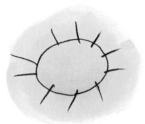

The mailbags are loaded onto airplanes. The bag with the letter to Grandma is flown to the post office in Grandma's town.

There is a letter carrier for each neighborhood in Grandma's town.

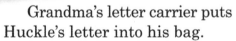

Grandma's letter carrier puts Huckle's letter into his bag.

Grandma is happy to receive a letter from Huckle, isn't she?

The Busytown School

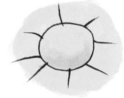

The bus driver is taking
these children to school.

Miss Honey is the schoolteacher.
She reads stories to her students . . .

and helps them learn to count to ten.

ABCDEFGHI JKLMNOPQR STUVWXYZ

Miss Honey asks Lowly to write the alphabet
on the chalkboard. Good work, Lowly!

Janitor Joe keeps the schoolhouse neat and clean.
He has come to wash the windows in the classroom.
Oh, dear! The pupils may be washed instead.
"Class dismissed," says Miss Honey.

Busy Housekeepers

Everyone helps out around the house.
Busy workers make a happy home.

A cook

A dish washer

A table setter

A wastebasket
emptier

A floor sweeper

A clothes
picker-up

A vacuumer

A bed maker

A tricycle painter

A fallen-leaf carrier

A window washer

A garden hoer

A garden waterer

A grass raker

A dirt mover

A lawn mower

A strawberry gatherer

Lowly Goes to the Medical Center

It's time for Lowly to have a checkup. The nurse at the medical center greets him. "Hello, Lowly," she says. "Dr. Lion will see you now."

"Your weight is just about right for such a skinny fellow," says Dr. Lion.

Dr. Dentist looks into Lowly's mouth. "Very good, Lowly," she says. "You have no cavities."

Now Lowly gets his eyes checked. "Lowly, tell me what you see on the eye chart," says the eye doctor. "Apples," says Lowly.

"You have very good eyes, Lowly," says Dr. Rabbit.

Dr. Lion checks Lowly's throat. "Open your mouth and say, 'Aaah,'" says Dr. Lion. "Very good!"

Nurse Nelly takes Lowly to
visit a patient with a broken leg.
Poor patient!
Nurses are good at taking care of people.

Lowly has an X ray taken.
"Your insides look good,
Lowly," says the X ray taker.

This is an ambulance. The ambulance driver
brings patients to the medical center when
they have to be taken care of in a hurry.

Keeping Busytown Clean

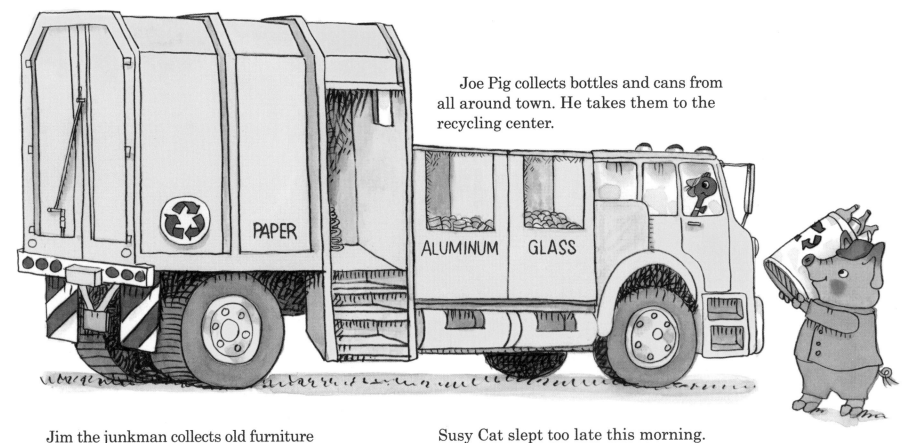

Pig Will is in charge of the Pig family's garbage. He takes the garbage from the kitchen and puts it outside in the garbage can.

Joe Pig collects bottles and cans from all around town. He takes them to the recycling center.

PAPER

ALUMINUM   GLASS

Jim the junkman collects old furniture in his junk truck.

Susy Cat slept too late this morning. Get out of bed, Susy!

REFUSE HAULED AWAY

Tincan Cat, the town sanitation worker, empties his garbage truck at the garbage dump.

Squish Cat squashes the garbage down with his squasher-downer.

Miss Kittycat uses her bulldozer to cover the garbage with dirt.

Grass and trees are planted. Someday the garbage dump will be a lovely picnic ground.

Brave Fire Fighters

Fire fighters must be ready for a fire at
any time. Sometimes the fire alarm bell rings
when they are sleeping. Wake up, fellows!
Slide down the pole and hurry to the fire!

The fire fighters hop into their fire engines.

The fire fighters attach a hose from the pumper truck to the fire hydrant.

A ladder truck

A pumper truck

They climb the ladders and put out the fire with water from their hoses. What brave fire fighters they are!

Fixer-upers

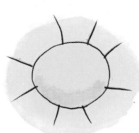

Mother Cat is having a bad day. Nothing seems to be working right. She has called many repair workers to fix things.

This man is replacing a broken window pane.

A TV repairman is fixing the television set.

A plumber is fixing the shower.

A locksmith is fixing a lock.

A telephone worker is fixing the telephone.

An appliance repairman is fixing the stove.

A roofer is fixing a hole in the roof.

A chimney sweep is cleaning the chimney.

This man is plastering the wall.

A painter is painting the walls.

A paperhanger is papering the walls.

An electrician is putting in new electric wires.

A furnace repairman is fixing the furnace.

A plumber is fixing a leaky water pipe. Hurry up, Mr. Plumber!

Lumber Workers

Many things are made of wood
We get our wood from trees.

Sometimes they cut a
tree down with a chain saw.

After they cut off the
branches, lumbermen cut
the tree trunk into logs.

Lumbermen cut down
big trees with their axes.

The logs are then pulled away to the sawmill
or put in a river to float downstream to a sawmill.

Workers at the sawmill use
giant saws to cut the logs into boards.

Carpenters use the boards to build
houses and many other things. Oh, dear.
This carpenter is not very lucky today.

Woodworkers

Here are many busy woodworkers making things with wood.

This worker is smoothing the top of a table with a sanding machine.

This worker is gluing the legs of a chair to the seat of a chair.

Helen is putting a wheel on the wagon she made.

Henry is taking a ride on the rocking horse he made.

George makes very fine beds to sleep in. He also makes chests to put clothes in.

Who is the busy box maker, I wonder?

A boat builder has built a fine rowboat and oars.
He is now going to row across the lake.

Barbie makes all kinds of toys with her jigsaw.

Wooden barrels can
hold all kinds of things.

Carpenters build wooden houses and barns.
Sometimes they hit their thumbs instead of
the nails with their hammers. OUCII!

This woodworker has just
made a toy sailboat.
What would you like to make?

Down on the Farm

Farmers work hard to feed us.
Farmer Haystack feeds corn to his
chickens so they will lay eggs for us to eat.

Mrs. Haystack gathers
eggs from the chickens' nests.

Farmer Pig feeds hay to his cow.
Cows give us milk to drink. MOOOO!

MILK

MILK

Farmer Fox plows his field.

Then he plants wheat seeds in the field.

When the wheat grows tall, he harvests the grain with his combine.

He takes the grain to the miller, who grinds it into flour.

Able Baker Charlie buys flour from the miller. He uses the flour to make our bread. YUM!

FLOUR
XXXX

The Streets of Busytown

Lots of people work hard to keep our neighborhoods clean. This worker is washing the street clean with his special machine.

Some workers sweep up litter with their brooms.

Other workers sweep the street with their street sweepers.

A hot dog man sells hot dogs.

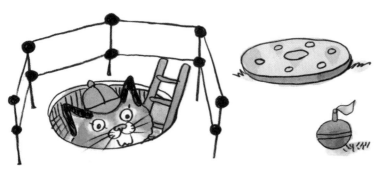

Some workers fix water pipes and electric wires which are buried under the street.

A worker digs into the pavement with his noisy jackhammer. He is going to fix a leaking water pipe.

A truck driver carries asphalt.

This worker is using the asphalt to fill up a pothole.

The newslady sells magazines and newspapers.

Hooray for the ice-cream man!

Cars and Trucks

There are many, many kinds of cars and trucks.
Lots of people use cars and trucks in their jobs.

The gardener uses his pickup
truck to haul plants and flowers.
He takes them to florists all
around Busytown.

Street lamp cleaners
sometimes drop things.
Be careful!

What does Pickles Pig
deliver in his pickle car?
Why, pickles, of course.

Trailer trucks haul things to stores all over town.
This truck is delivering fresh fruits and vegetables.

The cement mixer mixes cement
on the way to where a new building
is being built.

This is an armored car. It is used to
carry money from a bank. Robbers would
not be able to break into an armored car.

Have you ever
seen a cheese car
on the highway?

Lowly is a good
driver, isn't he?

At the Service Station

Garage workers take good care of our cars.

They fill our cars with
gas, oil, and water so that we
can drive wherever we need to go.

A garage worker uses a grease gun to help
all the parts under the car run smoothly.

When something is wrong with the motor,
the mechanic fixes it.

Sometimes a car breaks down on the road. The tow truck driver brings it to the garage to be fixed.

This worker is fixing a flat tire . . .

. . . and this one is washing a windshield.

Garage workers can make any car almost like new. Well—almost any car!

Railroad Workers

tank car

caboose

Rail yards are busy places.
Some railroad workers ride in a caboose.
The caboose is the last car on a train.

stationmaster

coal-powered
locomotive

oiler

conductor

signal

A hobo doesn't work, but he likes to ride in a boxcar.

hobo

engineer

The freight train engineer watches the signals. The signals tell him if he should stop the train or keep on going.

A worker fixes a broken signal.

The tower controller sees that all the trains stay on their own tracks.

control tower

cook

COACH

waiter

DINING CAR

wheel inspector

A conductor collects the passengers' tickets. The passengers are on their way to the seashore. It is a long trip, but there is plenty to eat in the dining car.

Would you like to ride on a train?

Around the Harbor

There is lots of work to do around a busy harbor. Would you like to work on a boat? A tugboat is small, but it can pull or push very heavy things.

tugboat captain

Oh, dear. The barge is on fire. But the fire fighters are putting it out right away.

fire fighters

buoy

fireboat

fisherman

forklift operator

This fisherman made a big catch today.

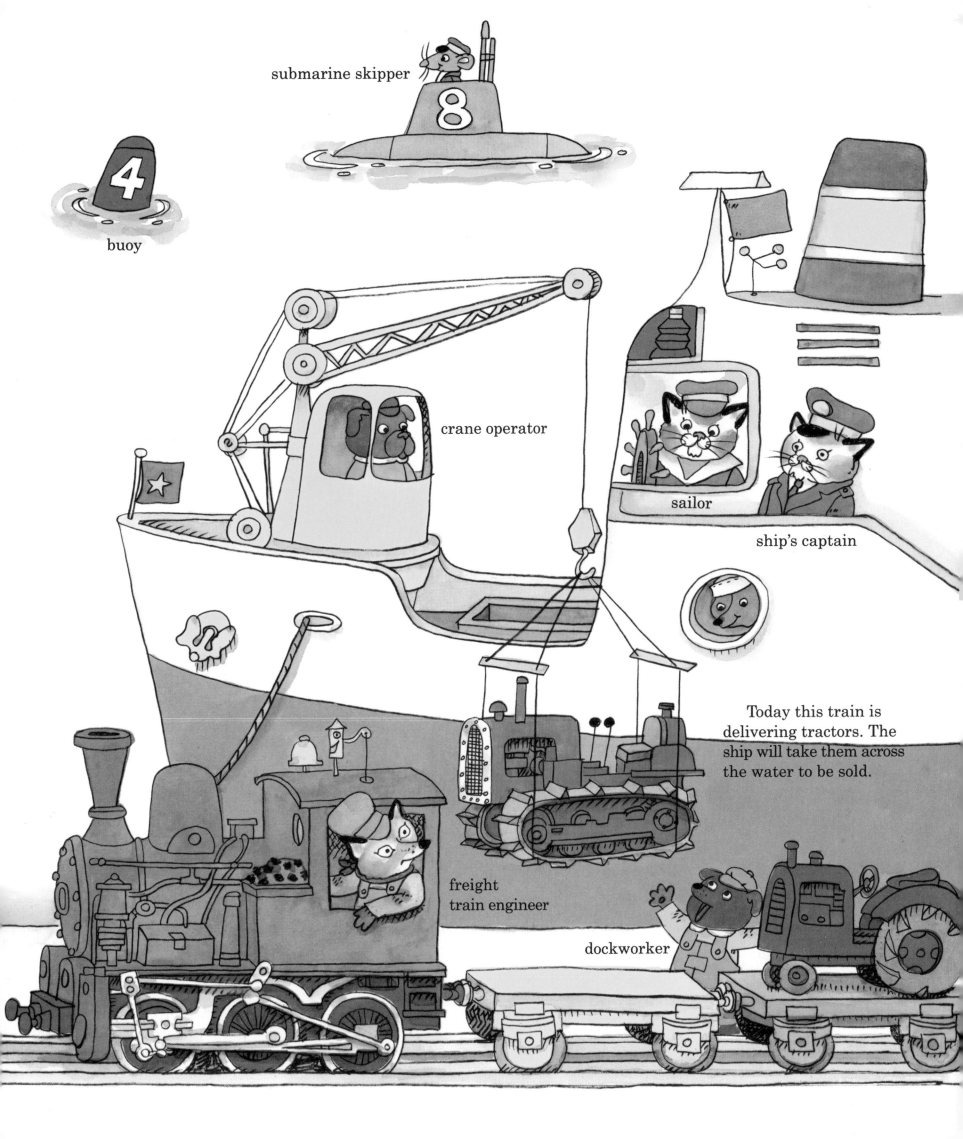

submarine skipper

8

4

buoy

crane operator

sailor

ship's captain

Today this train is
delivering tractors. The
ship will take them across
the water to be sold.

freight
train engineer

dockworker

At the Busytown Airport

An airport is a busy place. Many workers are needed to help the airplanes take off and land safely.

A jet pilot zooms by the jet control tower.

Air traffic controllers tell airplane pilots when they can take off and when they can land their planes.

A baggage handler takes baggage to a waiting airplane.

A check-in clerk welcomes passengers.

A taxi driver drives a passenger to the airport.

A helicopter pilot can fly straight up or straight down. He can even stay still in the air.

The pilot of this jet plane is giving Lowly a special ride.

The flight attendant takes good care of all the passengers.

A businesswoman is boarding the airplane.

Oh, dear! A businessman is losing his important papers.

This man is filling the fuel tanks.

FUEL

This man directs planes at the terminal.

At the Supermarket

Do you like to go to the supermarket? People work there every day so that we will have good things to eat.

The baker makes cakes, cookies, and bread.

The butcher cuts up meat and grinds hamburger.

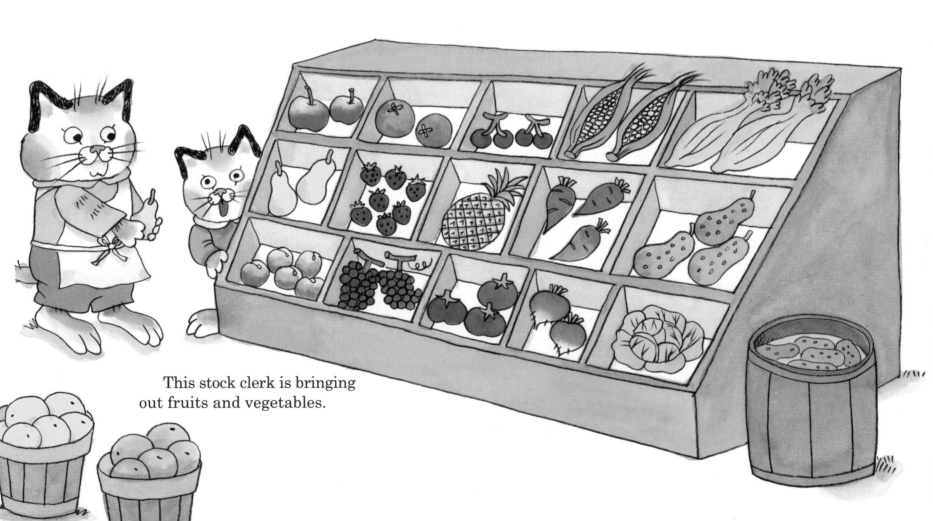

This stock clerk is bringing out fruits and vegetables.

The dairy case keeps butter, milk, and yogurt cold.

A food delivery has just come in by truck. Every day more trucks come to the supermarket.

This stock clerk has many cans of food to put on the shelves.

Shoppers pay the checkout clerk for the food they are buying.

Keeping Order in Busytown

Police officers do many different things during a busy day.

This police officer is telling these drivers when to stop and when to go.

Police officers take good care of lost children until their mothers come to get them.

Sometimes people park their cars where they are not supposed to. Police officers put parking tickets on those cars. The owners must then pay money to the town. That is called a fine.

Sergeant Murphy uses his motorcycle to chase speeding cars. Owners of speeding cars also have to pay money to the town, because speeding is very dangerous.

When there is an accident, it is a good thing to have a police officer around so that he can stop any quarrels.

Sergeant Murphy is going home to have dinner with his family. It is the end of a busy, busy day—in a busy, busy town. Good night, Sergeant Murphy!